MOON
LUNA

Aliana Reaches for the Moon

May you always reach for the moon!

Laura Roettiger

Written by Laura Roettiger
Illustrated by Ariel Boroff

Eifrig Publishing LLC
Lemont Berlin

At Eifrig Publishing, our motto is our mission —
"Good for our kids, good for our Earth, and good for our communities."
We are passionate about helping kids develop into caring, creative, thoughtful individuals who possess positive self-images, celebrate differences, and practice inclusion. Our books promote social and environmental consciousness and empower children as they grow in their communities.
www.eifrigpublishing.com

Printed in Canada

Published by Eifrig Publishing,
PO Box 66, Lemont, PA 16851, USA
Knobelsdorffstr. 44, 14059 Berlin, Germany.

For information regarding permission, write to:
Rights and Permissions Department,
Eifrig Publishing,
PO Box 66, Lemont, PA 16851, USA.
permissions@eifrigpublishing.com, +1-888-340-6543

Library of Congress Cataloging-in-Publication Data

Roettiger, Laura
Aliana Reaches for the Moon/
by Laura Roettiger, illustrated by Ariel Boroff
p. cm.

Paperback: ISBN 978-1-63233-196-0
Hard cover: ISBN 978-1-63233-197-7
Ebook: ISBN 978-1-63233-198-4

[1. Science - Juvenile Fiction 2. Creativity - Juvenile Fiction
3. STEAM - Juvenile Fiction

I. Boroff, Ariel, Ill. 2. Title

23 22 21 20 2019

5 4 3 2 1

Printed on 10% post-consumer recycled acid-free paper. ∞

Thanks to my daughters and the children of Carlos Fuentes Charter School in Chicago for my inspiration to reach for the moon.

~ Laura

To my Mom and Dad, I reached for the stars because of you and now I give you both the moon. Love, your youngest,

~ Ariel

Aliana lives in the Rocky Mountains, where the night sky holds more stars than you can dream of and the moon shimmers like gold.

The full moon lights up Aliana's whole world.

Each and every morning Papá says,
"It's a beautiful mountain day!
What do you have planned?"

Each and every morning, Aliana replies, “We’re exploring in the woods!” or “I’m reading an interesting book.” Today she is reading about the moon.
STARS
THE MOON IN THE NIGHT SKY.

Sometimes, using her favorite word, Aliana says, “I’m **creating** something special ... you’ll see when I’m done.”

Aliana has a big imagination and loves making things for her family, especially for her little brother Gustavo.

Some days Aliana creates things in her room.

Some days Aliana creates things outside.

Sometimes Aliana creates things at night.

animal

Today, Aliana is baking with Gustavo.

"Are we making these cuppie cakes for my birthday?"

"No, Gus, your birthday is still two weeks away. Besides, I'm working on a secret present for you. Be patient!"

Aliana's creativity is messy. She often leaves a trail of "treasures" around the house. Her room is the messiest of all.

Mamá and Papá are very patient for grownups. But...
Even the most patient grownups say, “Clean your room!”

"Creativity can be a little messy. I'm experimenting to make Gus's birthday surprise just right. You'll see."

Aliana's parents know their daughter is a clever girl with an amazing imagination. If she's creating something for Gustavo, they'll just have to wait.

Instead of finishing her project, Aliana spends her days outside with Gus exploring animal tracks and wildflowers in the woods. She notices things and shows them to Gus. *She teaches him how to notice things too.*

"Mamá, look what I made!"
"You always manage to see the beauty in everything," Mamá replies.

After a week of hikes in the woods, a day horseback riding, and two visits to the library, Aliana spends a day playing in her room.

At first, her parents think she is cleaning. *Sometimes parents can be silly.*

She's reading to discover how to create the perfect birthday suprise.

Aliana organizes pieces of quartz, crystals, and coins from her piggy bank into rows. Using marbles and several small mirrors, she plays with new shapes.

She selects two stem vases, two bottles from the recycling bin, and one very tall, skinny drinking glass. Aliana pours water into each one and carries them on a cookie sheet to her room.

Carefully, she drops coins, marbles, and pieces of quartz into the five containers. She tops each one with a crystal from her collection and steps back to look at her masterpiece.

During dinner Papá asks, “Did you do anything fun today?”

“My secret project for Gus is ready. You’ll see it tonight!” Aliana whispers.

After dinner, Gus and Aliana climb into their tree house to read books. Gus is excited because tomorrow is his birthday.

A·BC
ABCS
STARS IN THE SKY
Estrellas en el Cielo

Aliana is excited too. For weeks she has been planning and preparing for tonight.

The sun begins to set and the light in the tree house grows dim. Aliana waits for the moon to appear in the night sky. She's almost ready to show off her creation.

"Gus," she whispers. "Come with me."

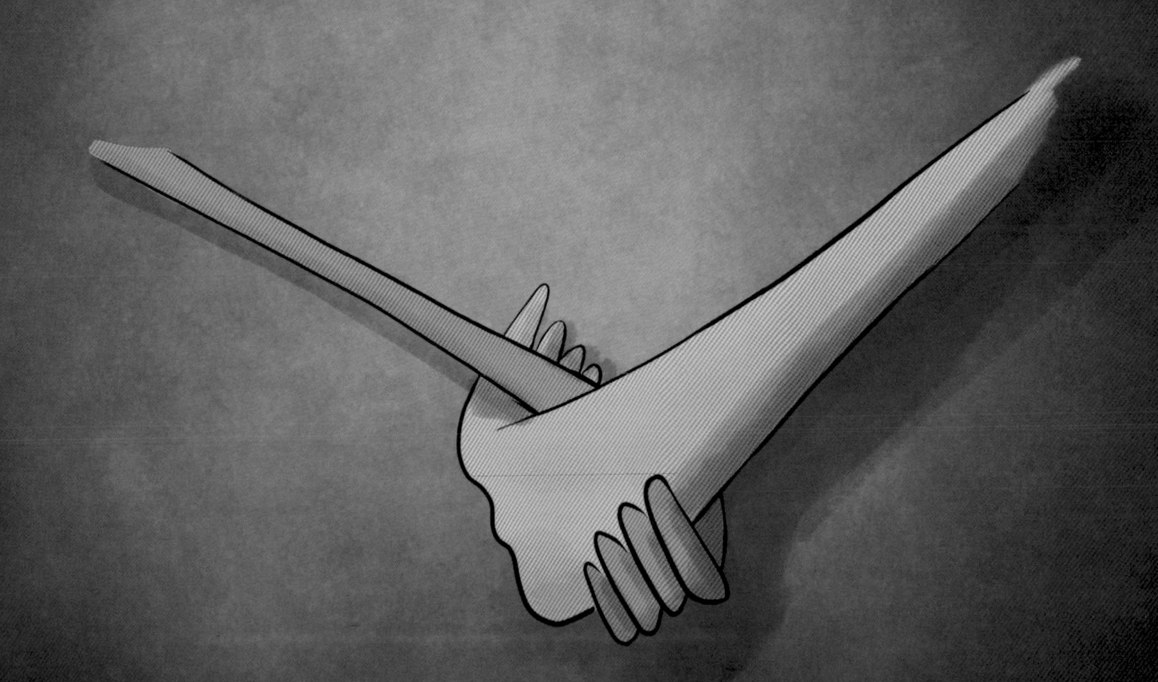

Aliana sees the moon reach the perfect spot ... and then, just like that it happens. Her experiment works. Aliana is beaming! Her face is almost as bright as the full moon.

The light from the moon shines through the skylight onto the creation in Aliana's room. In the window, Aliana's masterpiece sparkles and shimmers.

It doesn’t take much imagination to see five candles glowing.

"You made me a magical birthday cake!" Gus shouts.

"We have our very own astronomer!
I'm so proud of you," Papá says.

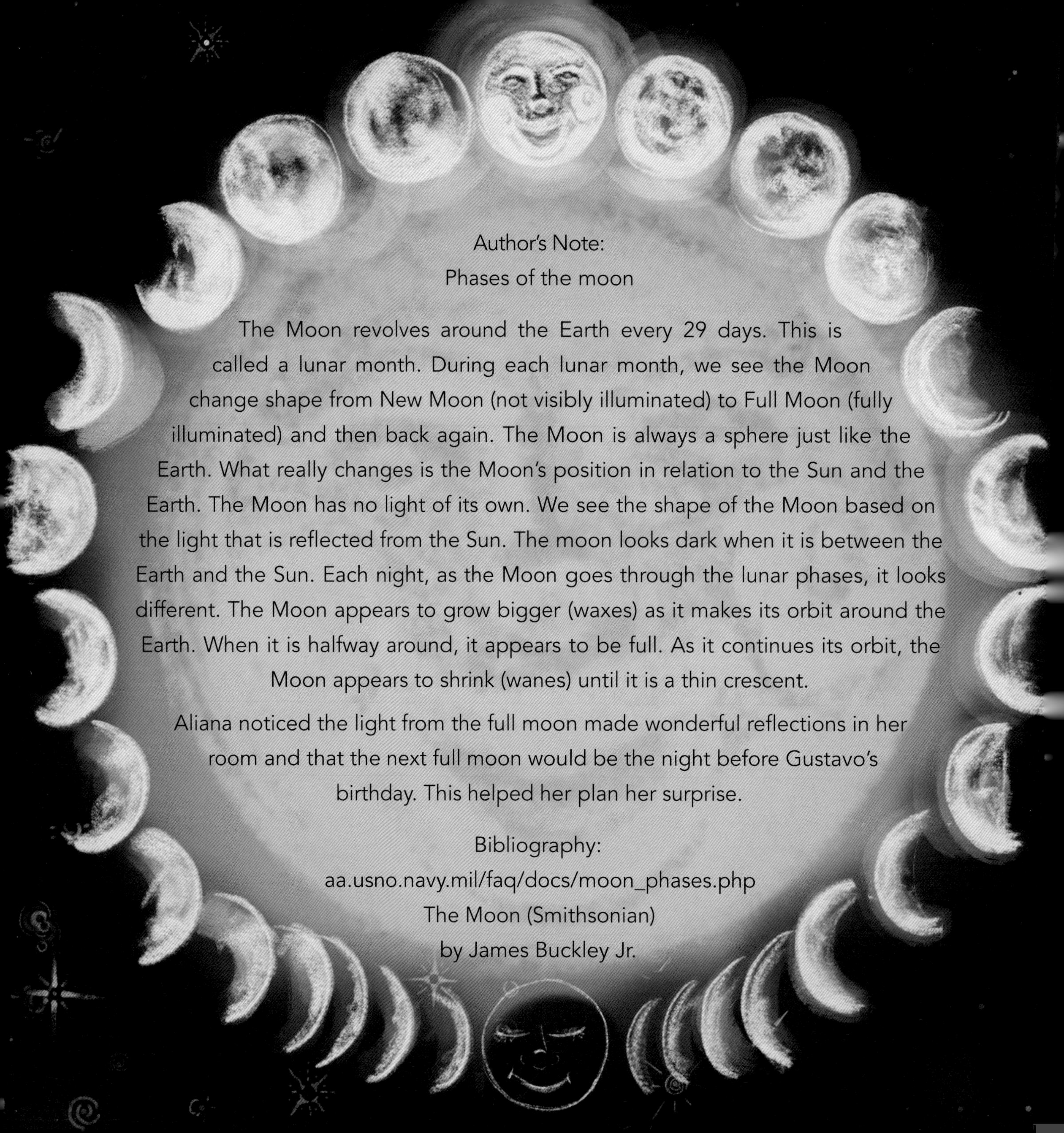

Author's Note:
Phases of the moon

The Moon revolves around the Earth every 29 days. This is called a lunar month. During each lunar month, we see the Moon change shape from New Moon (not visibly illuminated) to Full Moon (fully illuminated) and then back again. The Moon is always a sphere just like the Earth. What really changes is the Moon's position in relation to the Sun and the Earth. The Moon has no light of its own. We see the shape of the Moon based on the light that is reflected from the Sun. The moon looks dark when it is between the Earth and the Sun. Each night, as the Moon goes through the lunar phases, it looks different. The Moon appears to grow bigger (waxes) as it makes its orbit around the Earth. When it is halfway around, it appears to be full. As it continues its orbit, the Moon appears to shrink (wanes) until it is a thin crescent.

Aliana noticed the light from the full moon made wonderful reflections in her room and that the next full moon would be the night before Gustavo's birthday. This helped her plan her surprise.

Bibliography:

aa.usno.navy.mil/faq/docs/moon_phases.php
The Moon (Smithsonian)
by James Buckley Jr.

STARS